Bugs Meany i

"Trouble ha~ ~~~ ~~~~~, whispered Sally.

The Meany~ ~~~~~~~~~~~~~~~~~~~~~~~~

against you," O~~~~~~~~~~~~~~~~~~~~~~

pedia.

DISCARD

"This little do-gooder here was part of the gang that kidnapped me!" said Bugs.

"Tell him what you overheard," said Mrs. Meany.

"I heard the kidnappers say Encyclopedia

Officer Carlson said to Encyclopedia, "Is this some kind of prank?"

"Yes, sir," answered Encyclopedia. "It is."

Encyclopedia Brown

No. 3

Brown

Finds the Clues

By DONALD J. SOBOL

illustrated by Leonard Shortall

PUFFIN BOOKS
An Imprint of Penguin Group (USA)

PUFFIN BOOKS

Published by the Penguin Group

Penguin Young Readers Group, 345 Hudson Street, New York, New York 10014, U.S.A.

Penguin Group (Canada), 90 Eglinton Avenue East, Suite 700,
Toronto, Ontario, Canada M4P 2Y3 (a division of Pearson Penguin Canada Inc.)

Penguin Books Ltd, 80 Strand, London WC2R 0RL, England

Penguin Ireland, 25 St Stephen's Green, Dublin 2, Ireland (a division of Penguin Books Ltd)

Penguin Group (Australia), 250 Camberwell Road, Camberwell, Victoria 3124, Australia
(a division of Pearson Australia Group Pty Ltd)

Penguin Books India Pvt Ltd, 11 Community Centre,
Panchsheel Park, New Delhi - 110 017, India

Penguin Group (NZ), 67 Apollo Drive, Rosedale, North Shore 0745, Auckland, New Zealand
(a division of Pearson New Zealand Ltd.)

Penguin Books (South Africa) (Pty) Ltd, 24 Sturdee Avenue,
Rosebank, Johannesburg 2196, South Africa

Registered Offices: Penguin Books Ltd, 80 Strand, London WC2R 0RL, England

First published in the United States of America by Dutton Children's Books,
a division of Penguin Young Readers Group, 1995
Published by Puffin Books, a division of Penguin Young Readers Group, 2007

27 29 30 28

Contents

The Case of the Mysterious Tramp

His head bent low over the handlebars of his bike, Encyclopedia Brown rounded the corner of Maple Avenue like high-speed sandpaper.

It was three minutes before six o'clock of a summer evening. With a bit of luck and a following wind, Encyclopedia hoped to make it home on time for dinner.

Suddenly someone called his name.

"Leroy! Leroy Brown!"

Right off he knew it had to be a teacher calling. Only teachers and his mother and father called him Leroy.

Everyone else in the town of Idaville called him Encyclopedia.

He didn't look much like an encyclopedia, which is a set of books filled with all kinds of facts. Or even like one book.

People called him Encyclopedia because he had read more books than a bathtub full of professors. And he never forgot anything he read.

"Leroy! Leroy!"

It was Mrs. Worth, his old fourth-grade teacher. She was standing beside her car, looking very sad.

"I can't get it going," she said. "Can you help me?"

"I'll try," said Encyclopedia. He leaned his bike against a tree and raised the hood.

"Start her again, please, Mrs. Worth," he said.

The motor coughed and sputtered out.

"The trouble must be in the carburetor," said Encyclopedia, beginning to disappear under the hood.

He lifted off the air filter. Now he could reach the butterfly valve in the carburetor. He poked it open with his finger.

The motor roared to life when Mrs. Worth again tried to start it.

Mrs. Worth was delighted. When Encyclopedia returned to view, she thanked him over and over again.

"Golly, it wasn't anything," said Encyclopedia. "Just a stuck valve."

He smiled as Mrs. Worth drove off—till he looked at his watch. It gave him unsmiling news. It was past six o'clock, the Brown's dinner hour. He'd catch it for being late!

His mother put down a pot of boiled cabbage to stare at him. Dirt and grease from Mrs. Worth's motor coated him from ears to sneakers.

"Where have you been?" she asked, kissing the one clean spot on his cheek.

"Fishing," answered Encyclopedia.

"In an oil well?"

"The water was so dirty," Encyclopedia said quickly, "the goldfish looked like black bass."

He didn't mention Mrs. Worth's motor. He

seldom spoke to anyone, not even his parents, about the help he gave others. And he *never* spoke about the help he gave grown-ups.

His mother looked out at Rover Avenue through the kitchen window. Oddly, she hadn't scolded him for being late.

"Your father knows we are having corned beef and cabbage tonight," she said in a worried voice. "What could be keeping him?"

"Dad wouldn't miss his favorite dish without a good reason," said Encyclopedia. "Maybe he's chasing a dangerous crook or something."

Mrs. Brown looked even more worried.

Encyclopedia tried again. "Don't worry, Mom," he said. "Dad is the best police officer in the state. He'll be home soon."

Encyclopedia was right. As he was washing the back of his neck, he heard his father close the garage door.

A moment later Mr. Brown entered the house. He was a big, broad-shouldered man dressed in a police chief's uniform.

His uniform was the envy of every lawman in the United States. Although Idaville was like many other American towns, its police force was *un*like any other.

For more than a year, neither child nor grown-up had got away with breaking a law.

Hardened criminals had passed the word: "Stay clear of Idaville."

This was partly because the Idaville policemen were well trained, smart, and brave. But mostly it was because Chief Brown had Encyclopedia at the dinner table.

Chief Brown never whispered a word of how Encyclopedia helped him. After all, who would believe the truth?

Who would believe that a fifth-grader solved difficult cases while eating dinner in the Browns' red brick house on Rover Avenue?

Naturally, Encyclopedia never let out that he was the mastermind behind Idaville's war on crime.

So the name Leroy Brown was missing from the honor roll of the world's great detectives.

"I'm sorry to be late, dear," said Chief Brown as he sat down to eat. "A terrible thing happened this afternoon."

After he had said grace, he raised his head and looked at Encyclopedia. "Mr. Clancy, the plumber, was beaten and robbed."

"Was he badly hurt?" asked Mrs. Brown.

"He's in St. Mark's Hospital," Chief Brown said. "The doctors say he'll be all right. I'm afraid we'll never catch the man who attacked him."

"Why not, Dad?" asked Encyclopedia. "Didn't anyone see what happened?"

"John Morgan saw everything," said Chief Brown. "He's Mr. Clancy's helper. He was sitting in the truck when a tramp attacked Mr. Clancy."

Chief Brown unbuttoned his breast pocket and drew out his notebook. "I wrote down everything John Morgan told me. I'll read it to you."

Encyclopedia closed his eyes. He always closed his eyes when he did his heavy thinking on a case.

His father began to read what John Morgan had told him about the beating and theft.

"Clancy was driving the truck and I was sitting beside him. We had turned onto the dirt road near the Benson farm when the motor overheated. Clancy stopped, walked around to the front of the truck, and lifted the hood. As he took off the radiator cap, a tramp jumped out of the woods. The tramp struck Clancy on the head with a piece of pipe.

"Clancy fell over the radiator and slid down the front of the truck. I leaped out of the truck, but the tramp was already racing into the woods. He carried the pipe and Clancy's wallet. I let him go in order to get Clancy to the hospital right away."

Chief Brown finished reading and closed his notebook.

Encyclopedia opened his eyes. He asked but one question: "Did Mr. Clancy have an unusually large amount of money in his wallet?"

His father looked startled.

"Why, yes," he answered. "It so happened that Mr. Clancy had two hundred dollars in his wallet. He had just been paid for work on a new apart-

John Morgan knocked him out.

ment house. What made you think he was carrying a lot of money?"

"He had to be," said Encyclopedia. "Now you should have no trouble finding the man who struck and robbed him."

"No trouble?" said Chief Brown. "The woods come out on the railroad tracks. It's a sure bet that the tramp hopped a ride on a freight train. He's probably in Georgia by now."

"You'll find him where John Morgan lives—and the two hundred dollars besides," said Encyclopedia.

"Do you think John Morgan helped the tramp rob Mr. Clancy?" asked Mrs. Brown.

"No," answered Encyclopedia.

"Well, what do you think?" asked Chief Brown.

"I think that when Mr. Clancy stopped the truck in the woods, John Morgan saw his chance," answered Encyclopedia. "While Mr. Clancy was checking the radiator, John Morgan sneaked from the truck, knocked him out, and stole his wallet with the two hundred dollars."

"What about the tramp?" asked Chief Brown.

"There never was a tramp, Dad," said Encyclopedia. "John Morgan made him up. John Morgan robbed Mr. Clancy by himself and then drove him to the hospital."

Chief Brown rubbed his chin thoughtfully. "That could be what really happened," he said. "But I can't prove it."

"The proof is down in black and white," said Encyclopedia. "Just read over what John Morgan told you. He gives himself away!"

HOW DID JOHN MORGAN GIVE HIMSELF AWAY?

(Turn to page 89 for solution to The Case of the Mysterious Tramp.)

The Case of the Rubber Pillow

During the summer Encyclopedia ran a detective agency for children of the neighborhood. He opened his office every morning after his father left for work.

Encyclopedia always waited till his father drove off. He had no choice. His office was in the garage.

After his father left, he hung out his sign:

BROWN DETECTIVE AGENCY
13 Rover Avenue
Leroy Brown, President
No case too small
25¢ per day
plus expenses

Late in the morning Danny Landis hurried into the Brown Detective Agency. He laid a quarter on the gasoline can beside Encyclopedia.

"I want you to find my pillow," said Danny. "It's missing."

"I've seen a match box and a boardwalk, but I've never had to solve a pillowcase," said Encyclopedia thoughtfully.

"My pillow doesn't have a case," said Danny. "It's made of rubber. I blow it up on camping trips."

"Hmm," said Encyclopedia. "It gave you the air. When?"

"Half an hour ago," said Danny. "I think Bugs Meany stole it."

"Bugs?" Immediately Encyclopedia became serious.

Bugs Meany was the leader of the Tigers, a gang of older boys who caused more trouble than woodpeckers around a Maypole.

"I'll take the case," said Encyclopedia. "Let's have the facts.

"Early this morning," said Danny, "Dad and I were painting the wood on the front of our house—the three front steps, the porch railing and posts, and the front door. We painted everything white."

"Where was the rubber pillow?" asked Encyclopedia.

"It was hanging on the clothesline at the side of the house," said Danny. "After we finished painting, Dad went in the back to clean the brushes. I saw Bugs running away from the clothesline. He was carrying the pillow."

"Did your father see him, too?"

"No, worse luck," said Danny. "It will be my word against Bugs's."

Encyclopedia closed his eyes. For several minutes he did some deep thinking.

Then he said, "We've got to trap Bugs. We've got to catch him in a lie!"

"It won't be easy," said Danny. "He's smart enough to be the leader of the Tigers."

"That's not saying much," replied Encyclopedia. "Why, half of them have been left back so often they ought to start a football team. They could call themselves the Left Halfbacks. Come on."

The two boys rode their bikes to the Tigers' clubhouse, an unused tool shed behind Mr. Sweeny's Auto Body Shop.

Bugs was alone. He was practicing drawing aces from the bottom of a deck of cards.

"Scram," he said.

"I will when you return my client's pillow," said Encyclopedia.

"You stole my rubber pillow from the clothesline at my house half an hour ago," said Danny.

"*Rubber* pillow? Man, has this kid's mouth heard from his brain lately?" growled Bugs. "I've never been near his house in my life."

"Why don't you tell that to Danny's father?" said Encyclopedia. "He was behind the house. He must have seen you steal the pillow."

Bugs nearly swallowed the blade of grass he was

chewing. He recovered himself and said, "I've been right here all morning."

"Then you wouldn't mind going with us to Danny's house," said Encyclopedia. "You're going to have to speak with his father sooner or later."

"W-well, ahh, okay," mumbled Bugs. "But you lead the way. Remember, I don't even know where he lives."

Outside, Danny whispered, "My father went off fishing. My mother is at Grandma's. There's nobody at home."

"Don't worry," said Encyclopedia. "Bugs is far too cocky. He'll make a mistake."

The three boys rode over to Danny's house. It was a green stucco house with a white wood porch, door, and front steps.

"Go up and ring the doorbell," Encyclopedia dared Bugs.

Bugs kicked down the stand of his bike. He looked at Danny's house. He looked at Danny. He seemed to be getting up courage.

Suddenly the older boy made up his mind.

"Watch my style," he said.

He ran across the lawn and leaped over the three white wood steps. His heel struck the slate floor of the porch. He skidded but righted himself without having to grab the railing. He looked back at Danny and Encyclopedia and grinned cockily.

When he got no answer to the doorbell, Bugs walked a step to the window that faced onto the porch. He rapped on the glass.

"There's nobody home," he yelled to Encyclopedia. He left the porch, again jumping over the three steps.

"Your plan to trap him didn't work," said Danny.

"Oh, yes it did!" corrected Encyclopedia.

He went to Bugs and spoke into the bigger boy's left ear.

Bugs listened. His fists clenched and tightened. Pea green stars of anger seemed to shoot out his ears. Low, fighting sounds rumbled in his throat.

But he said, "Awh. . . ."

He leaped over the three white wood steps.

He got on his bike, a tame Tiger. Five minutes later he was back with Danny's rubber pillow.

"What did you say to him?" asked Danny, after Bugs had ridden off.

"Not very much. I simply pointed out his mistake," said the boy detective, and added, "In this case, actions spoke louder than words."

WHAT WAS BUGS'S MISTAKE?

(*Turn to page 89 for the solution to The Case of the Rubber Pillow.*)

The Case of Bugs's Kidnapping

Bugs Meany would have liked to get even with Encyclopedia by punching him in the eye four or five times.

But he didn't dare—for two reasons.

The first reason was the quick left fist of pretty, ten-year-old Sally Kimball. The second reason was Sally's right. It was even quicker than her left.

One day Sally had seen Bugs bullying a Cub Scout. "Stop it!" she had cried, hopping off her bike.

"Go powder your nose," Bugs had jeered.

Zam! went Sally's right.

Wham! went Bugs against the ground. He bounced up, red as a Jersey apple.

Sally's rights and lefts were a blur—*zing! zap! zam!* Bugs was something of a blur, too. He went up and down like a yo-yo—*wham! whap! whomp!*

Finally, Sally dusted his chin with an uppercut and left him panting on his back.

The news raced through the neighborhood. A *girl* had laid out big, bad Bugs Meany flatter than a smoked herring.

The next day Encyclopedia invited the new champion to join the Brown Detective Agency as a junior partner. Sally accepted on the spot, and Encyclopedia stopped worrying about Bugs Meany's muscles.

But Bugs didn't stop plotting. He just plotted farther behind Encyclopedia's back, and harder.

"Look out for him," warned Sally. "He's like a set of false teeth—always trying to get even."

"I sort of hope he keeps trying," said Encyclopedia. "Business would fall off without Bugs causing trouble."

"Trouble has just arrived," whispered Sally.

A police car drew up by the Brown Detective Agency. Out stepped Bugs, his mother, and Officer Carlson.

"The Meanys have brought a serious charge against you," Officer Carlson said to Encyclopedia.

"This little do-gooder here was part of the gang that kidnapped me!" said Bugs.

Encyclopedia and Sally stared at each other.

"Tell him what you overheard, dear," said Mrs. Meany.

"I heard the kidnappers say Encyclopedia Brown was going to pick up the money," said Bugs.

"I don't know what he's talking about," said Encyclopedia. "What kidnappers? What money?"

"Don't play dumb," sneered Bugs. "The ransom money."

"Start from the beginning," Officer Carlson said to Bugs.

"About five o'clock yesterday afternoon," began Bugs, "I was walking home from the clubhouse.

Bugs put on a brave look and continued.

I was minding my own business when somebody hit me on the head."

"He might have been killed!" said Mrs. Meany.

Bugs put on a brave look and continued.

"When I woke up, I was lying in a dark room without lights or windows."

"Could you hear anything?" asked Officer Carlson.

"Yeah," said Bugs. "I heard the kidnappers talking in the next room. They had telephoned my mother. She had agreed to pay one thousand dollars ransom money for my safe return."

Mrs. Meany broke in. "Around six o'clock last night I got a telephone call. The voice at the other end said to bring one thousand dollars to the old railroad station at nine o'clock that very night. I was not to call the police. A boy would meet me and take the money."

"That boy was Encyclopedia Brown, the pride of Idaville!" said Bugs. "I heard the kidnappers say he was to get one hundred dollars for picking up the ransom money."

"That's a lie!" said Encyclopedia.

"Quiet down," said Officer Carlson. "You'll have your turn. Go on, Bugs."

"When Encyclopedia didn't show up with the money," said Bugs, "the kidnappers figured he'd kept it all for himself. They got angrier every minute."

"I brought as much money as I could get together on such short notice to the old railroad station," said Mrs. Meany. "Nobody met me."

"I guess our little Mr. Smarty lost his nerve at the last minute," said Bugs. "But I didn't lose mine. I knew the kidnappers might kill me, they were so angry. I looked for a way to break out."

"My poor baby," said Mrs. Meany.

Bugs made a face and went on.

"I felt around the dark room where the kidnappers had put me," he said. "I found a crowbar. I thought I'd take the hinges off the locked door, but no luck. The hinges were on the other side of the door."

"How terrible!" sobbed Mrs. Meany.

"For Pete's sake, Ma, let me finish!" exclaimed Bugs.

He licked his lips and said, "I decided to break the lock and fight my way out. Before I could start, I heard the kidnappers coming toward the door. I planned to hit the first one who came into the room with the crowbar, take his gun, and shoot my way to freedom."

Bugs drew a deep breath. "I never swung the crowbar. The door was unlocked and pushed open hard. It swung into the room, knocking me down. I looked up. By the hall light, I saw a man pointing a gun at me."

Mrs. Meany gasped and wrung her hands.

"It looked like my number was up," said Bugs, rolling his eyes to heaven. "Instead, the kidnappers drove me to the place where they'd kidnapped me and let me go."

Mrs. Meany muttered about a miracle.

Officer Carlson said to Encyclopedia, "Is this some kind of prank?"

"Yes, sir," answered Encyclopedia. "It is."

Sally covered her mouth, stunned.

"It was probably one of the Tigers who telephoned Mrs. Meany to say Bugs had been kidnapped," explained Encyclopedia. "The rest is all made up."

"I'm no liar!" shouted Bugs. "I heard the kidnappers say you were hired to pick up the ransom money. You never showed up at the old railroad station. You got scared. My mother is right—I'm lucky to be alive!"

"I wasn't part of the kidnap gang," said Encyclopedia, "because there was no kidnapping. Except for one slip, you might have made everyone believe you, Bugs."

WHAT WAS BUGS'S SLIP?

(*Turn to page 90 for the solution to The Case of Bugs's Kidnapping.*)

The Case of the Boy Bullfighter

Charlie Stewart, who owned the best tooth collection in Idaville, slipped into the Brown Detective Agency. He wore bright red pants and a funny look.

Encyclopedia stared at his pal's red pants. "Who's chasing you? A lovesick fire engine?"

"How's your Spanish?" asked Charlie.

"Awful. Even Spanish moss gives me trouble," said Encyclopedia. "What's the problem?"

"My tooth collection has been stolen, including the flowered cookie jar I keep it in," said Charlie. "And I got bitten something fierce."

"One thing at a time," said Encyclopedia. "I thought you could reach into that cookie jar and

33

pull out a tooth without getting nipped, kind of like a snake trainer."

"I wasn't bitten in the cookie jar," said Charlie, turning around. "I was bitten here."

The seat of his red pants was missing.

"The teeth that bit me belong to a dog—a big, black dog," said Charlie. "And he understands only Spanish."

"I don't do well with dogs that understand only English," said Encyclopedia.

"You won't have to talk to the dog. Just get back my tooth collection," wailed Charlie.

He slapped twenty-five cents on the gasoline can beside Encyclopedia. "And while you're at it, find the seat of my pants!"

"Okay, but start at the other end," said Encyclopedia.

"You know Miguel Sebastian?" began Charlie. "He's eleven and lives on Hardiee Street. His father tosses the Spanish omelets at the cafeteria."

"Makes my Adam's apple jump just to think about them," said Encyclopedia, nodding.

THE CASE OF THE BOY BULLFIGHTER

"Half an hour ago I was going into Miguel's back yard with my tooth collection," went on Charlie. "He's putting on a show today."

"You tried to slip in free?"

"No, I thought if I got there before anyone else, I could give Miguel a gopher's tooth instead of the ten cents admission charge."

"What did Miguel say?"

"Something in Spanish, and *zoom!* His big, black dog caught me by the seat. Miguel was very polite. While he asked me if he could do anything, he took the cookie jar with the teeth. So it wouldn't break, he said."

"You were fighting all the time?"

"I was screaming bloody murder and running in place," said Charlie. "You should see that dog."

"Hmm," said Encyclopedia. "This case calls for extra equipment."

He filled a paper cup with chocolate drops left over from his mother's card party. Charlie borrowed a pair of pants, and the two boys went to see Miguel's show.

Charlie paid the admissions, and they found seats on the grass just in time. Miguel was about to start.

He was supposed to be a bullfighter, and his big, black dog was the bull. For horns, Miguel had tied two knives to the dog's head. To prove their sharpness, he sliced a banana on each knife.

The girls in the audience squealed in fright. Encyclopedia saw Sally in the front row. "She ought to be minding the detective agency," he thought darkly.

Miguel shook a red blanket. Like a real bull-fighter with a cape, he began to play the big dog. The dog had been trained to charge like a bull. It rushed the red blanket, teeth bared and knives flashing. Miguel spun aside.

"He spins better than a dime-store top," thought Encyclopedia. "But he's crazy! Those knives could hurt."

After ten or twelve passes, Miguel threw away the blanket he had been using. He took from his pocket a small piece of red cloth.

Miguel began to play the big dog.

Charlie muttered something that wasn't very nice. Encyclopedia could hardly blame him.

The small piece of cloth was the seat of Charlie's red pants!

Miguel used the piece of pants as a cape. Because it was smaller than the blanket, the knives passed dangerously close to the boy each time the "bull" charged.

After every charge Miguel stamped his foot, smiled at Sally, and shouted *oles* above the happy screams of the girls.

At last Miguel finished the act with a bow and ran into the garage. The show was over.

When most of the audience had left, Encyclopedia and Charlie started toward Miguel. The hero of the afternoon stood talking with Sally. The big, black dog sat between them.

Encyclopedia and Charlie slowed till they were traveling by inches. When Miguel glanced the other way, Encyclopedia tossed the dog a chocolate drop.

He fed the dog three more chocolate drops before he accused the boy bullfighter.

"You stole Charlie's flowered cookie jar with his entire tooth collection!"

"I did no such thing," said Miguel, calmly looking down his nose at the younger boys.

The dog growled. Encyclopedia eyed the big teeth and dropped more candies to help their friendship along.

"This afternoon you gave your dog an order in Spanish. It was to attack Charlie," said Encyclopedia.

"While that monster was hanging onto the seat of my pants, you took my tooth collection," said Charlie.

"I gave no such order!" said Miguel. "My dog did attack Charlie, all right. It is trained as a bull to go after anything red, like Charlie's pants. I pulled the dog off before Charlie was hurt. I wasn't even thanked!"

"You're lying!" said Encyclopedia.

"How dare you say Miguel did such a low thing," said Sally. "You ought to be ashamed. Miguel is no thief. He's brave and true!"

"The dog didn't attack Charlie because of the red pants," said Encyclopedia. "Miguel gave the order."

"Prove it," said Sally.

"That's easy," replied Encyclopedia.

WHAT WAS THE PROOF?

(Turn to page 91 for the solution to The Case of the Boy Bull-fighter.)

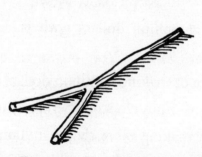

The Case of the Divining Rod

Sally jumped off her bike in front of the Brown Detective Agency.

"How much money do we have in the treasury?" she called.

Encyclopedia took the shoe box from its hiding place behind an old tire. He counted the money in it.

"Three dollars and eighteen cents," he said. "It's time we went to the bank."

"It's time we went to the beach," corrected Sally. "We can make a million at the beach."

"A million what? Footprints?"

"Take out the money and come on!" said Sally. "We can buy a divining rod for three dollars. We can make a million dollars with it. Maybe even more!"

The idea of making a million dollars had crossed the mind of Encyclopedia before. But he never thought of making *more* than a million.

"A divining rod?" he mumbled. "Say, isn't that a twig of hazel wood that's used to find underground water?"

"This divining rod doesn't find water," said Sally. "It finds *gold*."

Encyclopedia shoved three dollars into his pocket. He reached for his bike. "Tell me more," he said.

Sally explained how easy it would be to get rich as they rode toward the beach.

"Ace Kurash is selling the divining rods for three dollars apiece," she began.

"Ace Kurash . . . ?" Encyclopedia couldn't place the name.

"Last week Ace's father brought twenty rods back from the islands," continued Sally. "The first time out, Ace found a gold coin. It's worth ten dollars!"

Ace Kurash—suddenly Encyclopedia placed him.

Ace was seventeen. His father had a charter boat. Ace worked on it as a mate occasionally. Mostly he worked at the Children's Farm for stealing automobiles or television sets.

Encyclopedia and Sally reached the beach and parked their bikes. Around fifty boys and girls were standing near the old lighthouse on Pirates' Point.

Encyclopedia spied some of his gang among the crowd—Charlie Stewart, Billy and Jody Turner, Herb Stein, and Pinky Plummer. Bugs Meany and his Tigers were there, too.

In the center of the children were three tall boys in their late teens. One carried a basket filled with divining rods. The second carried a shovel. The third was Ace Kurash.

"A lot of you think I'm trying to cheat you,"

said Ace. "But I'll tell you this. Last week I took this divining rod out near the marina and found a buried gold coin."

Ace held up a coin in one hand and a divining rod—a forked twig—in the other.

"This coin is worth ten dollars," he announced. "If any of you had found it, you'd have paid off the price of a divining rod three times over!"

"Aw," grumbled Bugs. "Cut the chatter and let's see that hunk of firewood do its stuff."

"I don't blame you, kid," said Ace. "Doubt all you like—till you see it work with your own eyes. Me, I wouldn't pay three dollars on *your* say-so, either. So I'll tell you what I'm going to do. I'm going to find gold right here and now."

Ace held the forked twig with both hands. He bowed his head a second. Then he walked slowly down the beach.

Right behind him marched his two pals. The one with the shovel had it balanced lightly in his hands, ready to dig up sand the moment Ace gave the word. The other carried the basket of divining rods on his hip, ready to sell them like hotcakes when gold was discovered.

"If there is an ounce of gold under the sand here, I'll find it with my divining rod," promised Ace.

The children fell into step on each side of him. No one spoke a word. All eyes stared at the twig in Ace's hands.

"Lots of pirates used to come to this beach," said Ace. "Who knows how many treasure chests they hid around here!"

The boy with the shovel said, "See those sharp coral reefs by the lighthouse? You can guess the number of ships that got wrecked there. Plenty of gold and things washed up on the beach. Over the years, the ocean buried them."

The younger children hopped with excitement. It was true, all right. There must be tons of pirate gold lying around. Right under foot. Just out of sight!

Suddenly the twig in Ace's hands jumped and dipped.

The twig in Ace's hand jumped

"I got something!" he cried. He stopped by a log. "Here! Dig here!"

The boy with the shovel began to dig like crazy. The sand flew. Presently his shovel hit something—*clank, clank.*

Everyone pushed forward to see into the hole.

Ace lifted out an object shaped like a large brick. It was a foot long, six inches wide, six inches deep, and wrapped completely in dirty rags.

Ace unwrapped the rags. The sun shone on a brick—

"Gold!" screamed Ace. He raised the glittering, golden brick above his head with his right hand. He waved it for all to see. "I told you I'd find gold!"

He lowered the brick and covered it again with the rags.

"Okay, everyone," he said. "I'm not greedy. I'm willing to share. For three dollars you can buy a divining rod like mine. What works for me will work for you. Only three dollars."

"Just one to a customer," called the boy with the basket of forked twigs. "Get 'em while they last!"

"There's plenty of gold under the sand," said Ace. "Find it! Buy your mother a fur coat! Buy your father a new car!"

Encyclopedia watched Bugs Meany and his Tigers fight their way to the head of the line.

"Save your money," the boy detective told his friends. "Those twigs won't even make good slingshots."

HOW DID ENCYCLOPEDIA KNOW THE DIVINING RODS WERE FAKES?

(*Turn to page 91 for the solution to The Case of the Divining Rod.*)

The Case of the Bitter Drink

Mort Liveright was known throughout Idaville as Fangs. He was the only fifth-grader who could open a bottle of root beer between his front teeth.

One Thursday morning he came into the Brown Detective Agency and fell on the floor.

Encyclopedia was surprised to see Fangs in such bad shape. His face was very red; his well-known lower jaw hung down like a Christmas stocking; his cheeks were going in and out faster than a group of square dancers.

He reached an arm toward Encyclopedia. "Water," he said, "Water!"

Encyclopedia ran into the kitchen. He returned with a pitcher of water.

Fangs drank it dry. Slowly his cheeks stopped going in and out. His jaw tightened.

He stood up and explained: "I've been practicing."

"For what?" asked Encyclopedia, fearing the answer.

"I want to ride with the mayor in the Idaville Day Parade," said Fangs.

"Back up a little, please," said Encyclopedia. "What were you doing down there, huffing and puffing like the last dinosaur?"

"Did you ever drink castor oil mixed with vinegar and horseradish?" said Fangs. "I figured that if I could drink that, I could drink anything."

"Toughening up your tonsils, eh?" asked Encylopedia. "How come?"

"Every year the Daughters of the Pioneers hold Indian trials," said Fangs. "The boy who wins gets to ride in the mayor's car in the parade."

"Go on," said Encyclopedia. "I'll catch up."

"The Indian trials are made up of three contests," said Fangs. "Last year I won at boiling water. Melvin Hoffenberger won at setting up a tent. Then Melvin won the deciding contest—drinking the bitter drink."

"I begin to follow you," said Encyclopedia.

"In the old days," Fangs said, "an Indian youth couldn't become a brave till he swallowed a bitter drink without changing the expression on his face."

Fangs put a quarter on the gasoline can beside Encyclopedia. "I want to hire you," he said.

"You suspect Melvin cheated on his swallows?"

"He did something crooked last year," said Fangs. "The stuff we had to drink could clean a stove. But Melvin drank it down like pineapple punch. I want you to watch him at the Indian trials tomorrow."

"I'll watch him like a factory clock," promised Encyclopedia.

The next morning Encyclopedia rode over to Sally's house and explained the case.

"You keep an eye on the bitter drink," he said. "I'll be watching every move Melvin makes."

The Indian trials were held on the field behind the Veterans' building. When the two detectives arrived, the tent-pitching contest was beginning.

Encyclopedia looked around for Fangs. It was difficult to find him, because all the boys were dressed like Indians.

At the soda fountain outside the Veterans' building, Encyclopedia spied a small Indian. The Indian spat something into the trash can. It rang like a bottle top.

"Fangs," called Encyclopedia, hurrying over. "Why aren't you pitching a tent?"

"I'm saving myself," said Fangs. "It's too hot. Besides, Melvin will win easily. I've got to be at my best in the boiling-water contest. If I don't win that, the bitter-drink contest won't matter."

Encyclopedia had no trouble spotting Melvin among the twelve boys pitching tents. His tent was the first up.

Finally, all the tents were up. The boys moved into the shade of the trees to await the water-boiling contest.

Encyclopedia kept his eyes on Melvin. The champion sat down under a tree beside a towel and an ice bucket. First he filled his mouth with ice. Then he put some more ice in the towel. He held the towel to the back of his neck.

"He sure knows how to stay cool on a hot day," Encyclopedia thought admiringly.

Melvin sucked the ice and rested while the water-boiling contest was held out in the hot sun. All the boys in the contest used their hands only, except Fangs. He used his teeth, too.

The other boys tried to start a spark by knocking one stone against another. Fangs held a stone in each hand. He knocked against a *third* stone held between his mighty front teeth.

Sparks flew out of his mouth like a Chinese skyrocket. Before anyone else got the first weak flame, Fangs had a fire roaring under his kettle of water.

It was one victory apiece for Fangs and Melvin. The bitter-drink contest would decide the final winner!

Sally stopped by Encyclopedia. "The bitter

Sparks flew out of Fangs's mouth.

drink is ready," she said, shuddering. "It tastes like a mustard bath."

Only five boys dared try the drink. After one swallow, they dropped the cup and went leaping away as if gravity were out of style. The other boys hung back, looking at Melvin.

The champion calmly spat out his mouthful of ice. He wiped his hands on his towel and took the cup. He made his face as blank as a refrigerator door.

Then without changing expression he drained the cup.

"He isn't human!" moaned Fangs.

"You've got the strongest jaws here," said Encyclopedia. "Lock them together once you get the stuff down, and you'll win."

"Did you see something?" asked Fangs hopefully. "Did you see Melvin cheat?"

"Never mind," said Encyclopedia. "Just keep your face still and hold the drink in."

"Okay," growled Fangs, lowering his head determinedly. "Keep my face still, hold the drink in—I'll do it! I'll make them forget Hoover Dam!"

He seized the cup and downed it in two gulps. Then his mighty jaws locked, though his eyes popped in and out and he swayed and bounced around like a rope bridge.

"That's good enough to win," said Encyclopedia. "Only Melvin did any better, and he'll be ruled out of the contest after I speak to the judges!"

HOW HAD MELVIN CHEATED?

(Turn to page 92 for the solution to The Case of the Bitter Drink.)

The Case of the Telltale Paint

One afternoon Mrs. Carleton, who owned a flower shop, called Encyclopedia by a new name.

She called him a thief.

Encyclopedia was racing his bike down Prince Street when it happened.

He had sped past Mrs. Carleton's back yard with his head down. His eyes were on the road. He had not seen her struggling to her feet.

But she saw him whizzing off.

First her mouth opened so wide you could count her teeth. Then she started screaming as though Jesse James were getting away on a high-school horse.

"Thief! Stop, thief!"

Encyclopedia braked with all his might. He slammed to a stop like a near-sighted knight jousting the palace wall. Riding back to Mrs. Carleton, he felt his nose to see if it was bleeding.

Mrs. Carleton quieted down when she recognized Idaville's only boy detective.

"What were you speeding from?" she demanded, still suspicious.

"I'm in a bike race," said Encyclopedia. "It's twice around the block to see who clocks the fastest time. So far Herb Stein is leading by seven seconds."

"Oh," said Mrs. Carleton. "For a moment I thought you were the one who stole my purse."

"You were just robbed?"

"As I was getting out of my car," she said. "Somebody sneaked up behind me, grabbed my purse, and knocked me down."

"I didn't pass anyone," said Encyclopedia. "The thief must have run through one of the back yards."

"Then he's got clean away," said Mrs. Carleton.

"I'd better telephone for the police."

Encyclopedia straightened. It wasn't the moment for hiding his light.

"Excuse me," he said. "Perhaps you could use my professional services. My fee is only twenty-five cents a day, plus expenses."

Mrs. Carleton smiled. "All right. But your fee will have to wait till my purse is recovered."

"Is there anyone in the house?" Encyclopedia asked. "Anyone who might have seen what happened?"

"I live alone," said Mrs. Carleton. "Wait, Jim Krebs is somewhere around. I hired him to paint my orchid house today."

They found Jim in the tool shed, pouring white paint from one can into another.

"Hi, Mrs. Carleton," he said. "This can sprung a leak. So I'm putting the paint into this one."

Encyclopedia remembered seeing Jim, a boy of thirteen, hanging around the Tigers' clubhouse.

"Did you see who stole Mrs. Carleton's purse just now?" asked Encyclopedia.

"No," said Jim quickly. "I didn't see or hear anything. I've been in this tool shed the past few minutes."

"May I look around?" Encyclopedia asked Mrs. Carleton.

"Go right ahead," Mrs. Carleton said. "Jim, please help Encyclopedia all you can."

"Sure," agreed Jim's mouth. The rest of him looked as though he'd rather go over Niagara Falls on a salad plate.

Encyclopedia searched the tool shed. He even poked a stick into the can with the white paint. Satisfied that Jim had not stolen the purse and hidden it, he walked outside.

The path between the orchid house, which Jim had been painting, and the tool shed was about three hundred feet long. Drops of white paint from the leaking can had fallen in a straight line between the two small buildings.

"I was using the white paint when I noticed the leak in the bottom of the can," said Jim. "So I

Encyclopedia looked carefully at the drops of paint.

walked to the tool shed with the can. Those paint drops prove it. I didn't see or hear any thief."

"From any place on the path, you can see the spot where Mrs. Carleton was knocked down," said Encyclopedia. "You *must* have seen it happen."

"I didn't see anything," said Jim. "Leave me alone."

Encyclopedia went out to the path. He looked carefully at the drops of paint.

"Jim's telling the truth," he thought. "He couldn't be the thief. The paint drops show that he went straight from the orchid house to the tool shed."

Jim couldn't have had time to steal Mrs. Carleton's purse and run back to the tool shed, Encyclopedia realized. She would have seen him.

Then the boy sleuth noticed something strange about the drops of paint. They changed.

From the orchid house to about halfway along the path, the drops were nearly round. They had fallen about two feet apart.

But from the halfway point to the tool shed, the drops were narrow. They had fallen about eight feet apart.

"Hey, Encyclopedia! What are you doing?"

Encyclopedia looked toward the street. He saw some of the gang from the bike races— Herb Stein, Charlie Stewart, and Sally Kimball.

"Boy, we thought you'd crashed into a tree or something," called Herb.

Encyclopedia hurried over. He explained the reason for his failure to cross the finish line.

"Do you know who stole Mrs. Carleton's purse?" asked Sally.

"The thief got away," said Encyclopedia. "But Jim Krebs saw the whole thing. He won't admit it, though. I think he's scared the thief saw him and will hurt him if he tells."

"That's like Jim," said Charlie. "Bugs Meany won't have him for a Tiger. Bugs says Jim has only one stripe, and you know what color that is."

"He's so yellow he makes a canary jealous," said Herb.

"Stop being mean," said Sally angrily.

"It's not funny," agreed Encyclopedia. "However, Jim's fear did give him away. He suddenly got awfully frightened while he was carrying the leaky can of paint to the tool shed."

HOW DID ENCYCLOPEDIA KNOW?

(Turn to page 93 for the solution to The Case of the Telltale Paint.)

The Case of the Stolen Diamonds

Encyclopedia looked up from his book, *Diamonds for Everyone*. His mother stood in the doorway of his room.

"Did you know that diamonds are so hard they're used to drill stone?" he asked.

"I may need a diamond to drill my roast beef," said his mother. "It will be cooked as hard as stone if you don't come to dinner."

"Sorry, Mom," said Encyclopedia. He put the book aside, washed, and hurried to the table. He wanted to talk about diamonds.

His father, however, had a problem.

"The police chiefs from all over the state will be

here next week," said Chief Brown. "They chose Idaville for their yearly meeting."

"Are you worried about how to keep them interested?" asked Mrs. Brown.

"Exactly," said Chief Brown. "Every year there are speeches and more speeches. I want to do something different in Idaville."

"Why don't you have the chiefs solve a crime?" asked Encyclopedia.

"How can I?" asked Chief Brown. "There hasn't been an unsolved crime in Idaville in a year. Thanks to you know who."

"So commit a crime," said Encyclopedia.

"Did I hear you correctly, Leroy?" asked Mrs. Brown.

"I've been reading about diamonds," replied Encyclopedia. "Why not steal a diamond?"

"Mr. Van Swigget, the jeweler, has a diamond necklace," said Chief Brown. "It's worth fifty thousand dollars. Would you like to steal it for me?"

Encyclopedia shook his head and smiled.

"Make believe the necklace is stolen, Dad," he said. "Give the police chiefs all the clues. Then let them try to solve the case."

"Sort of a test, eh?" said Chief Brown thoughtfully. "By golly, you may have something there."

Between the roast beef and the butterscotch pudding, Chief Brown decided to put on the unusual event. Encyclopedia worked out the crime before going to bed.

In the morning his father went to see Mr. Van Swigget. The jeweler agreed to play a part in the make-believe crime. In fact, he was delighted to have a chance to test the best police brains in the state.

So it was that five days later thirty chiefs of police gathered in Mr. Van Swigget's office. Encyclopedia stood in the front of the room beside his father.

Mr. Van Swigget pretended to seem very upset.

"A diamond necklace was stolen this morning," he said. "It is insured for fifty thousand dollars. But money can't replace such a treasure!"

"Pardon me," said one of the chiefs. "What is that necklace on your desk, sir?"

Mr. Van Swigget lifted a necklace from his desk for all to see.

"This," he said, "is a copy of the stolen diamond necklace. As you can see, it is perfect in every way. Only it is made of glass. The thieves didn't bother with it. They knew it wasn't the real diamond necklace."

"Do you believe then that someone in your own store had a hand in the theft?" asked a chief.

"Yes, I do," answered Mr. Van Swigget. "The two necklaces are kept together in a safe when not on display. Had the thieves been unsure of which was the diamond necklace, they would have taken both. But they took only the real necklace."

Near Encyclopedia, one chief whispered to another: "Someone must have told the thieves which was the real necklace."

Mr. Van Swigget stood up. "Now, gentlemen," he said. "Please follow me. I shall show you how it happened."

From the office Mr. Van Swigget led the way into the hall. The floor of the hall was covered with stone. At the end of the hall was a marble staircase.

"The diamond necklace and the glass copy are kept in the safe on the second floor," said Mr. Van Swigget. "Shortly after ten o'clock this morning, I was bringing the fake necklace down to my office. Suddenly two masked men came charging up at me."

Mr. Van Swigget climbed the stairs. At the top he turned around. He started down, holding his hands before him. He was pretending to carry the glass necklace.

"One of the masked men grabbed the glass necklace," went on Mr. Van Swigget. "He fingered it, cursed, and threw it to the floor. At gunpoint the pair forced me back upstairs. I had to open the safe and give them the diamond necklace."

Mr. Van Swigget reached the bottom of the stairs.

Mr. Van Swigget pretended to carry the glass necklace.

"Gentlemen," he said to the police chiefs. "That is what happened. Are there any questions?"

"Are you sure that it would be impossible to tell the glass necklace and diamond necklace apart?" asked a chief.

"Not at a glance," answered Mr. Van Swigget.

Another chief asked, "Who knows about the glass copy besides yourself?"

"My store manager, Mr. Evers, and my secretary, Mrs. Zunser," answered Mr. Van Swigget. "They can tell the two necklaces apart. But they have been with me for twenty years. I trust them completely."

The chiefs had no further questions. Chief Brown stepped next to Mr. Van Swigget.

"In the showroom to your left you will find pencils and paper," said Chief Brown. "I ask you to write down your solution."

"Gosh, Dad," said Encyclopedia as the police chiefs passed into the showroom. "Do you think we made it too easy?"

"We'll soon find out," said his father. "But no

matter how many solve the case, it has made a big hit with everyone."

An hour later Chief Brown finished looking through the answers.

"You didn't make the case too easy," he told Encyclopedia. "Only four of the thirty chiefs named the person behind the theft and told where the diamond necklace could be found."

DO YOU KNOW?

(Turn to page 94 for the solution to The Case of the Stolen Diamonds.)

The Case of the Missing Statue

The news spread through the neighborhood. Linda Wentworth, the famous movie actress, was coming to Idaville!

A crowd of excited children hurried to the waterfront house that the star had rented. Soon three cars drove up.

The last car carried newspaper reporters. The middle car carried Miss Wentworth's hairdresser and Miss Wentworth's luggage. The first car carried Miss Wentworth and her bodyguard, a big man called Rocco.

As the actress got out, Bugs Meany shoved past Encyclopedia and stepped out in front of the children.

"Stand aside, I'm about to be discovered," he said, whipping a comb through his hair. 'I'll be the hottest thing in picture-making since the washable crayon. Just watch me go places!'"

Bugs went places—up. Rocco lifted him by the shirt collar.

"Sorry, kid," said Rocco. He moved the toughest Tiger out of the way like a gooseneck lamp. "No autographs."

"Some other day, darlings," cooed Miss Wentworth. She blew kisses to the children and swept into the house.

"What is Miss Wentworth doing in Idaville, Dad?" Encyclopedia asked at the dinner table that evening.

"It does seem a bit strange," said Chief Brown. "Her new picture, *The Stolen Lamb*, opens tomorrow in theaters across the country."

"You'd think she would be going from city to city to build up interest in the picture," said Encyclopedia.

"According to the newspaper, she brought the

lamb used in the picture," said Mrs. Brown. "It's a silver statue covered with jewels and worth a hundred thousand dollars."

"I read that," said Chief Brown. "In the movie the lamb is stolen, and Miss Wentworth nearly is killed helping the hero find it."

"I'll have to go see the movie," said Encyclopedia, as the telephone rang.

His father took the call in the kitchen. When he stepped back into the living room, he wore his gun.

"I have to go over and see Miss Wentworth," he said. "The statue of the lamb has been stolen from her bedroom."

"May I go along?" cried Encyclopedia.

"Ordinarily I'd say no," answered Chief Brown. "But this case is different. It may teach you something about movie people. Let's go."

Sitting beside his father in the car, Encyclopedia asked, "What did you mean by the remark about movie people?"

"Movie people," said Chief Brown, "will do

anything to get their names and pictures in the news."

"Do you think the statue *wasn't* stolen?" exclaimed Encyclopedia. "Why would Miss Wentworth make it up? Just to get a news story to help her picture, *The Stolen Lamb?* That would be plain dishonest!"

"Actors aren't like other people," said Chief Brown. "They don't care about what is right or wrong as long as they get attention."

Encyclopedia felt angry at his father for talking like that. He sat in silence during the rest of the ride to Miss Wentworth's house.

The actress herself answered the door.

"Darling, how good of you to come," she said. "What a simply dreadful thing to happen!"

"May we see the room where the statue was kept?" asked Chief Brown, after he had introduced Encyclopedia.

The actress led the way through a group of newspaper reporters and up the flight of stairs to her bedroom. At the door, Rocco, her bodyguard, joined them.

"I haven't touched anything," said Miss Wentworth. "I know you wonderful policemen want everything left just as it was."

"Thank you," muttered Chief Brown.

Miss Wentworth's bed stood against one wall. The sheets had been torn off and knotted together. One end of the sheets was tied to the foot of the bed. The other end hung out the window to within four feet of the ground.

"I kept the statue on this table," said Miss Wentworth. "The thief must have hidden some place in the house. When we were all downstairs, he must have slipped in here and stolen the statue. I saw it was missing when I came upstairs to change my clothes for dinner."

"I was coming from the garage when I saw a huge man carrying the statue drop to the ground," said Rocco. "I ran up to him, but he knocked me down and got away."

Encyclopedia wondered how anything smaller than a freight train could knock down Rocco.

"The thief was a very strong man to climb down the sheets with the statue," said Chief Brown. "It must weigh a lot."

"About a hundred pounds," said Rocco.

Chief Brown looked around the room carefully. Then he asked Encyclopedia to step into the hall. Father and son agreed upon their next move.

Encyclopedia was to use the sheets to climb to the ground, as the thief had done.

But from the window, Encyclopedia saw Bugs Meany standing on the sidewalk below. He was still dreaming of becoming a movie star, for his hair was parted and he wore sunglasses.

"Hey, Bugs," called Encyclopedia. "Want to help Miss Wentworth? Climb up the sheets. She's right up here."

"*Rabadabadoo!*" sang Bugs, grabbing hold of the end of the sheets. "I knew she couldn't get me out of her mind."

Bugs started up. The bed, to which the other

Bugs Meany was standing on the sidewalk below.

end of the sheets was tied, creaked loudly. Suddenly it pulled away from the wall.

Encyclopedia heard something fall down, something that had been caught between the bed and the wall. It was a fountain pen. Chief Brown picked it up.

"Is it a clue, darling?" asked Miss Wentworth.

"It's the clue that solves this case," said Chief Brown.

Encyclopedia had never seen his father look angrier.

Bugs Meany appeared at the window. It was his big moment. But Miss Wentworth didn't even know he was there.

She was looking nervously at Chief Brown.

"The statue of the lamb was never stolen," he said. "Where have you hidden it, Miss Wentworth?"

HOW DID CHIEF BROWN KNOW
THE ROBBERY WAS FAKED?

(Turn to page 95 for the solution to The Case of the Missing Statue.)

The Case of the House of Cards

During the week that Encyclopedia's mother stored her old sofa in the garage, Benny Breslin came around regularly.

Benny was a wonder at making things. It was widely held that he would grow up to become a famous builder of bridges and skyscrapers—if he could keep awake.

Benny and Encyclopedia liked nothing better than to talk about bridge building. Benny talked while lying on the old sofa. It helped him "think like a bridge," he said.

He usually stayed awake till they had worked out the bending moment of a cantilever. At that point, he rolled over and started snoring.

Benny stopped by the day after the Salvation Army finally carted off the sofa. He stared at the empty place in the Brown garage. Disappointment dripped from his face.

"Sorry," said Encyclopedia. "Maybe we could talk about flagpole watching. That might help you keep upright."

"Never mind," said Benny. "I just wanted to invite you to my birthday party Monday."

"Gosh, thanks, I'd love to come," said Encyclopedia, though he remembered the strange ending of Benny's birthday party last year.

Then, the children had played softball after lunch, and Benny had hit a triple. But he had fallen asleep while waiting on third base. The game had to be called, because no one dared to wake him. After all, it was *his* party.

By Monday, Encyclopedia had polished up his black shoes till they shone like the seat of a bus driver's pants. He biked over to Sally's house, and together the partners rode to Benny's.

"What's your present?" asked Sally.

"A book about bridges, naturally," said Encyclopedia. "What's yours?"

"Two decks of playing cards. Each card has a picture of a different famous building."

The other children had brought presents in line with Benny's interest in construction. There were eight boys and eight girls. Encyclopedia knew them all except a boy named Mark Plotz.

Mark kept to himself. He seemed more interested in the tool chest Mr. Breslin had given Benny than in making friends. Encyclopedia learned from Herb Stein that Mark was new in Idaville.

"His parents are friends of Benny's parents," said Herb. "I tried talking to him, but it's like crossing a mule with an otter. All you get are mutters."

When all the presents had been fingered, Benny's mother served lunch. Then the games began.

The first game was a scavenger hunt. Mrs. Breslin gave each child a paper bag, a pencil, and a list of eight things to collect.

Encyclopedia's list read: a safety pin, a flashlight, a 1960 penny, a green crayon, an ace of hearts, a bar of pink soap, a toothbrush, and a soup spoon.

"I'd rather finish the softball game we started last year," Fangs Liveright whispered to Encyclopedia. "We only got in three innings before Benny went into his standing snooze at third base."

"Me, too," said Encyclopedia. "Where will I find a bar of pink soap?"

An hour later Encyclopedia was hunting through his mother's medicine chest for the soap when Sally shouted from the street.

"Come back to Benny's house!" she cried. "His new tool chest has been stolen!"

Encyclopedia flung down his half-filled paper bag. "Benny's best present!" he said, jumping on his bike. "Poor guy!"

Benny looked close to tears when Encyclopedia entered the Breslin living room. The other children stood around dazedly, except Mark Plotz. He seemed in pain. Encyclopedia noticed he was limping.

Mrs. Breslin was talking on the telephone. Encyclopedia could hear her telling somebody about the theft.

The tool chest was missing from its place on the floor beside the other presents.

"Who discovered the theft?" asked Encyclopedia.

"I did," said Mark. "I needed a queen of hearts for the scavenger hunt. I remembered the cards Benny got for his birthday. I came in here to borrow the queen."

"That's when you noticed the tool chest missing?"

"Missing, nothing!" exclaimed Mark. "I saw a big kid with it in his hand. He ran to that window and jumped out."

"You didn't try to stop him?"

"Sure I tried," snapped Mark. "I ran for him, but I hit my shin against the coffee table and fell

Mark said, "Boy, my leg still hurts."

flat. Boy, my leg still hurts. When I got up, the thief was being driven off in a black hot rod."

"That's what woke me up," said Benny. "Mark was leaning out the window shouting, 'Thief!'"

"Where were you sleeping?" asked Encyclopedia.

"On the sofa," answered Benny. "I needed a jack of spades for the scavenger hunt. I opened Sally's present. I got interested in the pictures of the buildings on each card, and I began building a house with them."

On the coffee table, which stood about a foot in front of the sofa, was a five-story house built of cards.

"After I used up all the cards, I got sleepy," said Benny. "The next thing I knew, Mark was shouting, 'Thief!'"

"Did you see a black car on the street?"

"No," said Benny. "But I heard a car. By the time I got to the window, it had turned the corner."

"I didn't see the thief's face," said Mark. "But

he wore a leather jacket with the letter L on the back."

"That makes him one of the Lions, that gang of tough teenagers on Woodburn Avenue," said Sally.

"Maybe," said Encyclopedia. "Let's look outside, Sally."

The two partners stopped before the open window the thief had reportedly used. Encyclopedia studied the bushes below it. He found several branches were broken.

"The thief must have hurt himself jumping out," said Encyclopedia. "I bet he didn't get far. He probably hid the tool chest some place, and he plans on returning after dark for it."

"Gee whiz," said Sally. "Do you think that's how Mark hurt his leg? Is he the thief?

"Of course," said Encyclopedia. "It was in the cards all the time."

HOW DID ENCYCLOPEDIA KNOW
MARK WAS LYING?

(*Turn to page 96 for the solution to The Case of the House of Cards.*)

Solution to *The Case of the Mysterious Tramp*

John Morgan said that Mr. Clancy walked around to the front of the truck and raised the hood.

He described how "Clancy fell over the radiator and slid down the front of the truck" after being struck by the tramp. Then he himself "climbed out of the truck."

But he said he had been sitting in the front seat. So he saw the attack through the windshield.

Impossible!

The hood of the truck was raised, remember?

All John Morgan could have seen through the windshield was the hood!

Chief Brown recovered Mr. Clancy's money. The guilty John Morgan was sent to prison.

Solution to *The Case of the Rubber Pillow*

Bugs claimed he had never been to Danny's house.

Yet he knew the porch railing, the steps, and the front door were just painted and still wet.

How had he given himself away?

By: 1) jumping over the steps getting on and off the porch, instead of mounting them; 2) righting himself without touching the porch railing after he skidded; and 3) knocking on the glass window rather than on the front door when no one answered the doorbell.

Obviously, Bugs didn't want to get fresh white paint on his hands and shoes!

Solution to *The Case of Bugs's Kidnapping*

Bugs said, "I thought I'd take the hinges off the locked door, but no luck. The hinges were on the other side of the door."

But then he said the door "swung into the room, knocking me down."

Impossible!

Doors swing toward their hinges. So the door of the locked room would have swung into the *hall*, not into the room.

When trapped by his error, Bugs confessed. The kidnapping was a fake.

Bugs had dreamed it up to get even with Encyclopedia.

Solution to *The Case of the Boy Bullfighter*

Miguel lied when he said the dog attacked Charlie because of his red pants.

Dogs can't be trained to attack the color red, because dogs are color blind!

So the big dog couldn't have known whether Charlie had red or yellow pants on.

Therefore, Miguel must have ordered the dog to attack.

When reminded that dogs are color blind, Miguel gave back the tooth collection.

He also returned the seat of the red pants, which Charlie's mother sewed back as good as new.

Solution to *The Case of the Divining Rod*

Encyclopedia realized Ace had painted a brick with a couple of dollars' worth of gold paint and buried it. Then he pretended to find it with the divining rod.

The other children were ready to believe the divining rod really worked. However, the brick Ace supposedly "found" under the sand was a foot long, six inches wide, and six inches deep.

Ace could not have lifted it above his head with one hand if it had really been made of solid gold.

A solid gold brick of that size weighs nearly three hundred pounds!

Solution to *The Case of the Bitter Drink*

Melvin used the ice to cool himself in the heat of the day—and for something else.

He kept ice in his mouth to freeze the taste buds of his tongue.

With his taste buds deadened, he couldn't taste a thing.

So he had no trouble at all in drinking the bitter drink!

Solution to *The Case of the Telltale Paint*

Jim said he "walked" to the tool shed with the leaking paint can. But the paint drops on the path told otherwise.

Halfway toward the tool shed the drops "were nearly round. They had fallen about two feet apart."

But on the last half of the path, the drops "were narrow. They had fallen about eight feet apart."

That meant that on the last half of the path, Jim was covering more ground between the falling drops—he was *running*. (The drops were being flung instead of dropping straight down and therefore were "narrow.")

Encyclopedia knew that at the halfway point, Jim had seen the thief. Becoming frightened, he had run into the tool shed and hidden.

When faced with the evidence, Jim broke down. The thief was quickly arrested, and Mrs. Carleton's purse was recovered.

Solution to *The Case of the Stolen Diamonds*

In the test thought up by Encyclopedia, Mr. Van Swigget played the part of the criminal mastermind.

He had hired the masked men to rob him—of the wrong necklace!

Remember how the masked man on the stairway had thrown the supposedly glass necklace away? Had it truly been glass, it would have broken on the stone floor.

But the "glass" copy that the police chiefs saw on Mr. Van Swigget's desk wasn't broken. It was "perfect."

So the necklace on his desk, which had been thrown to the floor, had to be the diamond necklace. Diamonds, being harder than stone, wouldn't have broken on the stone floor.

The masked men had stolen the glass necklace!

Thus in the make-believe theft Mr. Van Swigget not only kept the diamond necklace. He would have collected the fifty thousand dollars' insurance money besides!

Solution to *The Case of the Missing Statue*

Miss Wentworth said she hadn't touched anything in the bedroom since the theft.

Her bed was pressed so tightly against the wall that a fountain pen was trapped in between. And the sheets were tied to the foot of the bed and run out the window.

The thief, "a huge man," carrying the heavy statue of a lamb, had supposedly climbed down the sheets.

Yet when Bugs Meany, a boy, had climbed up the sheets, what had happened?

His weight had *pulled the bed away from the wall!*

Had the huge man really climbed down the sheets, the bed would have been pulled away from the wall when Chief Brown and Encyclopedia first saw it.

Miss Wentworth admitted the statue hadn't been stolen.

The fake robbery was a stunt to get publicity for her new picture, *The Stolen Lamb.*

Solution to *The Case of the House of Cards*

Encyclopedia knew that Mark had hurt his leg jumping out the window with the tool chest.

Mark couldn't have hurt the leg as he said—hitting it against the coffee table.

The five-story house of cards was still standing on the coffee table. If Mark had hit the table hard enough to knock himself down, the house of cards would have crashed!

When faced with this fact, Mark confessed.

He had stolen the tool chest and hidden it in the yard next door. Returning to the living room, he had made up the part about seeing the thief escape.